EGMONT

We bring stories to life

First published in Great Britain in 2006 by Dean,
an imprint of Egmont UK Limited,
239 Kensington High Street, London W8 6SA

Thomas the Tank Engine & Friends

A BRITT ALLCROFT COMPANY PRODUCTION

Based on The Railway Series by The Rev W Awdry

Photographs © Gullane (Thomas) Limited 2006

© Gullane (Thomas) LLC 2006

Thomas the Tank Engine & Friends and Thomas & Friends are trademarks of Gullane Entertainment Inc.
Thomas the Tank Engine & Friends is Reg. U.S. Pat. & Tm. Off.

ISBN 978 0 6035 6236 5
ISBN 0 6035 6236 1
1 3 5 7 9 10 8 6 4 2
Printed in Singapore.

Thomas, James and the Red Balloon

The Thomas TV Series

DEAN

It was summer holiday time on the Island of Sodor. But not for the engines. For them it was the busiest time of the year. They worked hard carrying holidaymakers all over the Island.

One day The Fat Controller sent Thomas to pick up something very special from Brendam Docks.

"What have you got there?" said Percy.

"A balloon," replied Thomas.

"A party balloon?" asked Percy excitedly.

"No," said Thomas. "This is a very special balloon."

He chuffed away, leaving Percy feeling very curious indeed.

Thomas hurried along and soon arrived at an airfield. Hot air was pumped into the balloon. There was a big basket underneath and people were climbing into it.

James arrived with some coaches. "What is that?" asked James.

"It's a hot air balloon," explained Thomas. "Holidaymakers can ride in it!"

Then, as if by magic, the hot air balloon rose silently up into the sky. The engines could see the people inside looking over the edge of the basket.

"What if it takes our passengers away?" huffed James. "What would happen to us then?"

"I hadn't thought of that!" replied Thomas.

James chuffed away, and Thomas felt very worried.

The balloon could be seen by everyone on the Island of Sodor. Donald gazed at it for so long, he nearly ran into the back of Douglas.

"It's a floating basket with people in it!" exclaimed Donald.

"Whatever will they dream up next?" said Douglas.

James and Thomas were waiting at a level crossing for Bertie to cross the line. Thomas was still worrying about the balloon.

"It does look nice," said Thomas. "But what if it takes all our passengers?"

"Passengers belong on trains!" said James crossly. "Not in silly balloons!"

Then something big and round and red drifted straight towards them.

James and Thomas were not pleased.

"Oh no!" cried Thomas. "You saved it!"

The barrier lifted and Thomas puffed crossly away.

"I didn't mean to!" groaned James. "Now it's bound to take our passengers."

When James arrived at the station, The Fat Controller was waiting on the platform. "Well done, James!" he said. "The balloon's pilot told me that he was in trouble until you let out your burst of steam."

"I wish I hadn't done it," said James, sadly. "Now the passengers will ride in the balloon instead of the train."

The Fat Controller laughed. "These holidaymakers are coming to ride in the balloon! But they will need a ride home – in a train!"

James was delighted. He whistled happily and went off to tell Thomas the good news.

The Fat Controller was right. The engines were busier than ever. They took holidaymakers to and from the airfield all day long.

Thomas and Bertie sometimes raced each other to get passengers to the airfield first.